SILVER

By Gloria Whelan
Illustrated by Stephen Marchesi

A STEPPING STONE BOOK

Random House New York

Library of Congress Cataloging-in-Publication Data:
Whelan, Gloria. Silver / by Gloria Whelan ; illustrated by Stephen Marchesi. (A Stepping stone book) SUMMARY: Even though her puppy is the runt of the litter from her father's prize sled-racing dog, ten-year-old Rachel plans to train him to become a champion racer and determines to track him down when he mysteriously disappears. [1. Dogs—Fiction. 2. Sled dog racing—Fiction. 3. Alaska—Fiction.] I. Marchesi, Stephen, ill. II. Title. PZ7.W5718Si 1988 [Fic]—dc19 87-26612 ISBN: 0-394-89611-4 (pbk.); 0-394-99611-9 (lib. bdg.)

Manufactured in the United States of America 1 2 3 4 5 6 7 8 9 0

For Rachel Barr

1.

In Alaska, where I live, there isn't much daylight in the winter. It's dark when the school bus picks me up in the morning and it's dark when the school bus brings me home in the afternoon. In the middle of the morning, when it finally gets light, we all look out of our classroom window to see if the mountain is out.

The mountain is Denali, the biggest one

in North America. Although it's nearly a hundred miles away from us, when the sky is perfectly clear, there it is. The sun makes the white snow-covered peaks shine. There is snow on top of Denali all year round. In summer, when you are outside without even a sweater on, picking nagoonberries while the mosquitoes are biting and the shooting stars and poppies and wild roses are blooming, there is still snow on Denali, so that you can never really forget winter.

My name is Rachel. I'm nine years old. I live halfway between Anchorage and Fairbanks. In summer my father is a carpenter. In the winter he travels all over Alaska competing in dog-sled races. My mother has a beauty parlor right in our house. She cuts the hair of everyone within fifty miles of us, even Mr. Rafer. He has so little hair, Mom says she hates to take his money.

When I get home from school I like to go into the room my mother uses for a beauty parlor. After all the cold and snow and darkness outside, the room is brightly lit

and warm from the hair dryer. It smells good, too. Mom makes me cocoa when I come in, and I drink it while her ladies have their coffee and tell Mom all their secrets. Mom says she could write a book. Dad says he hears more news from Mom's ladies in one afternoon than he reads in the newspaper all year long.

After I've warmed up, I go outside and play with the sled dogs. That's because I don't get to play with my friends much. In our part of Alaska there aren't many houses. The nearest girl my age lives fifteen miles away. Her name is Mary Sue. Sometimes she spends the night with me and sometimes I stay with her. Mary Sue's dad plays guitar in a country music band. Her mother sings with the band. Mary Sue can tap-dance and twirl a baton, and she says she might be famous one day. I like Mary Sue all right, but she won't play outside if it's raining or damp or there's a wind blowing, because it takes the curl out of her hair. And in Alaska that's nearly all the time. Worse than that, she's afraid of big dogs. When she comes to our house we have to keep all the dogs shut up. That's not easy, because my dad has forty-eight of them.

Some of Dad's dogs are Siberian huskies. Some are just mutts that have been bred to be good racers. When the dogs hear me coming they begin whining and barking. The noise is so loud you can hardly hear yourself think. My dad likes me to play with the dogs. He says it's important for them to get used to being around people. Touchy dogs don't make good racers.

My dad's favorite dog is Ruff. She's a lead dog. Although Ruff is gentle when you play with her, as soon as you put on her harness and fasten her to the sled's traces she outruns all the other dogs. Dad says Ruff's great-grandfather was a wolf and that's why she's so courageous. There are lots of wolves around here. We can hear them howl at night. Sometimes there is an answering howl from Ruff, so I guess what Dad says must be true.

Dad hasn't been racing Ruff because she's expecting puppies any day. She's in a pen by herself. When I visit her, she lets me put my arms around her and curl up next to her.

Then she licks my face with her rough tongue.

When I got home from school yesterday, two good things happened. Mom and Dad told me I could go with them to Anchorage to see Dad race, and for the first time in

weeks the mountain came out of the clouds and you could see the sun shining on the snowy peaks. Dad was already putting dog boxes in the pickup truck. We would take fourteen dogs with us, even though Dad wouldn't use them all. You have to have extras in case one gets a lame foot or something. In the house, Mom was cooking

up a couple of gallons of moose stew with fish and lard for the dogs to eat on the trip.

It smelled awful, so I hurried out of the kitchen and went up to my room to pack my good parka and boots. February is the best time of year to go to Anchorage because it's when they have the Fur Rendezvous. Everyone calls it the "Rondy." It started when all the trappers used to come to Anchorage to sell their fur pelts; now it's what everyone does to keep from going crazy in the long Alaskan winters.

2.

We got to Anchorage just before dark. The sun was setting, making the snow on the Chugach Mountains purple and gold. The hot-air balloons, blue and yellow and green, were drifting around over the city. Because Cook Inlet is on one side and the mountains are on the other, there are only two roads out of Anchorage—one going south and one going north. If you want to head somewhere

else, you have to use the sky. So everyone is always going up in balloons or planes.

This was my second Rondy, but I was only five when I went to my first one, so that hardly counted. We drove right to the Coopers' Motel. Mom and Dad always stay there. It's cheap and the Coopers like mushers—that's what everyone calls dog-sled racers. Most motels aren't too happy to have you check in with fourteen hungry, yelping dogs.

Right away Mom began thawing the frozen moose stew in the bathtub. Dad brought the dogs in to check their paws. The motel room was so small you couldn't move without tripping over a dog. Mary Sue would have hated it. Bender and Slim and Pilot were on one bed. Red and Elf and Sally were on the other bed. Tiger had gotten into Dad's suitcase and was chewing on his socks. Lightning and Laggard were trying to climb over Mom and get into the bathtub. The rest of the dogs were snuffling Mr. Cooper, who was standing in the

doorway looking around the motel room with a big smile on his face.

"Jim," he said to Dad, "your dogs are looking better every year. Real lively. But where's Ruff?"

"She's about to have puppies," Dad said. "Nothing we planned." Dad meant someone left the gate open between kennels at the wrong time. "Then you won't have her for the Iditarod?" Mr. Cooper asked.

"Nope," Dad said. "But that's not going to stop me. I wouldn't miss that race for anything."

The Iditarod is the most famous dog-sled race of all, right across Alaska, from Anchorage to Nome. It's more than a thousand miles, along frozen rivers and empty fields of ice and snow. Once I asked my dad what it was like to be all by himself with only the dogs for company and with nothing around but wind and snow.

He said, "It's like walking into a white room that is so long and so wide and so high you can't tell where it begins or ends."

Twice now Dad has won some of the prize money. In last year's Iditarod he was fifth and got enough winnings to cover his entry fee and put a down payment on our new pickup.

After the dogs were fed, Dad put them outside in the truck, two to a box so they could keep each other warm. "All right," he said. "Mr. Cooper will keep an eye on the dogs for us. Let's see something of the big city."

We headed for the mall. Right there in the middle of it was this huge stuffed brown bear about ten feet tall. I didn't think anything could be larger than that stuffed bear, but Dad said he saw a live brown bear in the woods once and it *looked* twice as big. Then we spent a lot of time just going up and down the aisles of a supermarket, looking at all the fancy food. Mom said, "One day I'm going to leave the dogs home and just come down here and fill the truck with pineapples and oranges and little tiny shrimp. Why are we living out in the middle of nowhere when I could be shopping here every day?"

Dad said, "Those pineapples don't taste as good as our wild blueberries, and the shrimp can't touch the salmon and trout I catch in our own stream." He knew Mom didn't mean anything by her complaining. Whenever he suggests moving into Anchorage or Fairbanks, Mom says, "Just send me a postcard and tell me how you like it, because I'm staying right here." She says that in big cities you have to keep your shoes on and your door locked.

Dad dragged us out of the supermarket and into Sears to look at dumb things like generators and chain saws. Then we had burgers and milk shakes. We went back to the motel to get a good night's sleep. We didn't. The motel was full of mushers, and all night long there were about a thousand dogs yapping at one another.

3.

In the morning, when we looked out of our motel room window, we saw that fog from Cook Inlet had rolled into town, making everything invisible. Then, by the time we were dressed and the dogs had eaten their morning moose stew, the fog was gone. But it had done a wonderful thing. All the trees in town were covered with ice crystals. It looked like someone had wrapped every

trunk and branch and twig in glass. The
sun shining on the ice made the whole city
glitter.

We put the dogs into the truck and drove
into town. Anchorage was crowded. The
native Eskimos had flown down from their
villages. They were all dressed in beautiful

parkas trimmed with seal and wolf fur. Everywhere you looked something was happening. There was Eskimo blanket tossing. Four Eskimos hold on to the corners of a blanket while the Eskimo on the blanket gets thrown up into the air. People say Eskimo hunters used to do that

so they could be high enough to see a bear on the horizon, but to me it just looks like fun. Hot-air balloons had come from all around the state, and there were snowshoe and ski races. Anchorage is a big city, but on Rondy days it's more like a small town because everyone is so friendly. I guess it just feels good to be out of the house in the middle of winter.

When we got to the chute—that's the starting line for the race—Dad was so excited Mom had to help him get all the dogs out of their boxes. The Rondy race only lasts for a couple of hours, not like the Iditarod, which goes on for weeks. Still, it's a championship race and a lot of your friends are there watching and rooting for you to win.

Mom and Dad harnessed up the dogs. Bender and Red were trembling and shaking the way they do before each race. Lightning and Laggard kept yanking this way and that, tangling everything up. Dad told me to put my arms around Sally. She was going to be the lead dog. "Talk to her, so she won't get impatient. I wish we had Ruff here. She doesn't have a nervous bone in her body."

The other mushers were harnessing their dogs. All the racers wore a number on their backs so you could tell who everyone was. The course ran right through the middle of Anchorage. Hundreds of people were lined up along the way to cheer for their favorite team. The racers want to beat each other, but they're friends, too. One of them was warning the rest that there were sharp ice crystals along the course. He said the dogs ought to have their booties on to keep their paws from being cut.

I helped Mom and Dad get the booties out. By the time we had finished putting them on the dogs, the race was ready to begin. The dogs were so eager you could hardly hold them back. "Hike!" Dad cried, giving the signal that started the dogs, and they took off. A few minutes before, Dad had been laughing and talking with everyone. Now, what you could see of his face with the ski cap pulled down was serious and determined. Dad said he only raced for the fun of it, but Mom said he lied through his teeth when he said that. She said he would rather win a race than land a five-pound trout, and that was saying a lot.

After the mushers were on their way, we teamed up with a couple who had a car. They drove us to a place on the trail where we could see the sleds go by. Dad came racing along in fifth place. I waved and yelled at him. So did Mom, who was shouting, "Go for it!" If Dad saw us, he didn't let on. He was gaining on the sled ahead of him. I heard him shout "Trail!" That means "move over." Then he was in fourth place.

Mom and I got to the finish line long before the sleds did, so we had plenty of time to worry about how Dad would do. Mom started combing my hair and arranging my parka and looking around for my mittens. You can always tell when she's jumpy, because she starts straightening me up. Finally I was so neat I couldn't stand it any longer, and I went over to talk to Mr. Cooper, who always comes to the races.

"I got a feeling your dad's going to do just fine today," he said. "One of these days I'll bet you'll be out there behind a sled yourself. Don't forget it was a lady racer who won the Iditarod last year."

Up until that very second I had never thought about being a musher, but as soon as I heard what Mr. Cooper said, I knew I wanted to race sled dogs. That's what I was thinking when I heard everyone begin to cheer. The first sled wasn't my dad's, but the second one was! Second place was the best he had ever done at the Rondy races. There wasn't a whole lot of prize money, but with the dogs doing so well, things looked good for the Iditarod. Mom and I hugged

each other and then we were throwing our arms around Dad. I was even hugging and kissing the dogs. It was right then that I decided I would ask for one of Ruff's puppies. I would train it to be the fastest lead dog in Alaska.

4.

As soon as we got home I asked Dad if I
could have one of Ruff's puppies when they
were born. "Someday I'll give you a puppy
from one of our other dogs," Dad said. "But
Ruff is such a good lead dog, her puppies are
too valuable to give away." I guess I must
have looked pretty unhappy because Dad
said, "I'll think about it, Rachel. Right now
I have other things on my mind."

What he had on his mind was the Iditarod. It always takes place the first Saturday in March and that was only a few weeks away.

Dad was practicing every day. Some days he and the dogs would go forty or fifty miles. None of his customers called anymore to see when he could come and build something for them. They knew that this time of year all he cared about was the big race.

When it started getting dark out, Mom and I would listen for Dad calling out "gees" and "haws"—right and left—to the dogs on his way home. Sometimes you could hear the jingler—the bells mushers use to get the dogs excited and make them go faster. Dad would walk into the house and surrounding him there would be a sort of cold breeze left over from the outside. His teeth would be chattering and his hair and eyebrows all frosted over. Even his mustache would have little icicles hanging from it.

Right on my tenth birthday and just two days before Dad was to leave for the Iditarod, Ruff had five puppies. "Because they were born on your birthday," Dad said, "I'll give you one of the puppies—the runt of the litter. He probably won't make much of a racing dog."

My pup had one blue eye and one brown eye. He had soft, downy fur the color of shiny coins. "I'm going to call him Silver," I said.

Ruff and her puppies were out in the shed. I went there about twenty times a day to check on Silver. I didn't care that he was small. I would give him extra food. I'd tell him stories about all the famous dog races. And as soon as he was old enough, I'd start training him, just like Dad trains all his puppies, by having Silver pull a little wheeled cart.

When it was time for Dad to leave for Anchorage for the start of the Iditarod, our whole house was turned upside down to get him ready. On his sled Dad carried

snowshoes and a sleeping bag, extra clothes for himself, his food, and tons of food for the dogs. He even had to carry a little gas stove to heat their food, because in the cold everything freezes. Besides the moose stew, Mom made the dogs honey balls—an icky mixture of ground beef, oil, honey, and vitamins.

Dad took along some postcards I had addressed to me. The racers stop at checkpoints to pick up extra food. If one of their dogs is too tired or has hurt itself, the racers can make arrangements to get a new dog from a checkpoint. Dad promised to write to me on the postcards and leave them at the checkpoints, where someone could mail them back to me. That way I'd hear from him all through the race.

After Dad left, Mom and I listened to the radio reports on the race every day. Even my teacher knew Dad was in the Iditarod. She would show the class on the map just where the racers were, like when they got to

Shaktoolik and had to cross miles and miles of frozen sea.

My dad was the only parent in my school who was in the race, so all the kids were really impressed. Mary Sue was so jealous of all the attention I was getting, she wore her pink satin tap skirt and her tap shoes to school, even though it was ten below zero out. I was really glad when our teacher, Mrs. Proofer, told Mary Sue the shoes made so much noise clacking around the room she wasn't to wear them to school again. "There's a proper time and place for everything, Mary Sue," Mrs. Proofer said. She says a lot of things like that.

Every afternoon, when the school bus brought me home, I would gulp down my cocoa and hurry out to tell Silver how the race was going. When Silver heard me coming he would give sharp little welcoming barks and whimpers. I saved some of my own food for him—oatmeal or an egg (which I don't like that much

anyhow) from breakfast and some meat or
fish from dinner. Silver would gulp down
the food. Then he would lick my face and
hands to thank me. I think Mom knew what
I was doing, but she didn't say anything.
She just gave me bigger helpings.

I don't know if it was all the extra food (I even sneaked him my vitamin pills) or the stories I told him about the Iditarod, but Silver began to catch up to the other pups. Mom said sometimes that happens with runts. I began to worry that if Silver got too strong, Dad might take him back. Mom said Dad would never do that. "He'll be proud of what a good job you're doing. Considering what you've been giving Silver to eat, though, my cooking should get some of the credit!"

I was brought up with sled dogs and I always liked playing with them, but until I had Silver, one dog was sort of like another. Silver was all mine. I got to know all about him—how his tail had a funny bend in it, how he rolled over so you could scratch his stomach, and how, even though the other puppies were bigger than he was, he pushed and yelped until he managed to get as much milk from Ruff as they did.

Silver knew a lot about me, too, because I

told him. I told him how even though she doesn't say anything, Mom worried a lot about Dad when he was racing. I told him Mary Sue said I was her best friend and when she went to New York City and got on television she would invite me to come and spend a weekend in her skyscraper condo. I told Silver I liked Kevin best of all the boys in my class because he brings such great things to school—like rocks that are a million years old and a deer mouse in a little house he made just for it. I told Silver I thought I had the largest feet of any girl in my class. Silver just licked my face. Dogs make good listeners.

5.

Each morning, when I woke up, the first thing I thought about was my dad. It seemed like he had been away forever instead of just three weeks. The Alaskan spring had already started, but you could hardly tell. One day the chinook, the soft wind from the ocean, would blow, turning the snow into wet puddles. The next day a cold wind would stir up a snowstorm. Then the mountains turned into great white humps and school would be closed because the buses couldn't make their way through the snowdrifts. When I was stuck at home I would get out the postcards Dad had sent and read them over. Most of them were just a few scrawled sentences about the race. That's because he was always in a hurry, but on one of them he told how he had seen the northern lights flashing in the sky. The whole sky was different colors, he said, just like a hundred rainbows.

One afternoon, just before school was out, it started snowing. We were all tired of the snow, and everyone groaned. It had been over three weeks since Dad had left. I was wondering if it was snowing out on the trail when Mrs. Brace, our principal, announced over the loudspeaker that the Iditarod was over. My dad had come in third and was already on his way back from Nome. Everybody cheered and congratulated me, even Mary Sue. In the Iditarod, third place is really good.

I couldn't wait to tell Silver, but it took forever to get home from school. First there was a moose in the middle of the road and the bus driver, Mr. Jenkin, had to honk his horn about ten times to chase it away. Then

the snow was so heavy that Mr. Jenkin could only creep along. He started singing "Amazing Grace," like he always does when the driving is bad.

By the time the bus dropped me off it was late. So instead of going into the house for cocoa, I just ran to the shed. I wanted to tell Silver about Dad coming in third. I knew Mom and the ladies would have the radio on and know all about it already. When I got to the shed I saw that the door was open. I had forgotten to latch it that morning when I brought Silver his cereal. Sometimes when I'm in a hurry I do dumb things. Ruff was yelping wildly and straining on her leash. I could see only four puppies. I counted again. Silver was missing. My heart flip-flopped like a fish when Dad catches it and throws it on the grass. I ran outside. There were large tracks sort of like dog tracks in the snow, but all our dogs were either with Dad or in their kennel. I forgot about the cold and the snow and hurried along in the direction the tracks took. All I could think about was finding Silver.

The tracks followed the curve of a little river where my dad catches salmon and trout in the summer. A thin coat of ice lay like white lace along the edge of the water. I crossed an open patch where my mom and I pick huckleberries in July. A snowshoe hare, all white but for the beginnings of his brown summer coat, bounded across my path. Then a flock of startled snowbirds flew up as though someone were scattering bits of white paper into the sky. The trail led into the woods, where the fir trees were frosted with snow. Their branches looked scary, like giant white arms reaching out for me. I didn't know where the tracks were leading or whose they were, but I was sure whatever it was had taken Silver.

I was getting to be a long way from our house. I began to wish I had told my mom so she could have come with me, but I couldn't turn back because the snow was beginning to fall harder and the tracks would be covered over in no time. Then I might never find Silver.

The tracks suddenly turned into a lot of tracks circling a big old spruce tree. At the base of the tree something had dug a cave into the roots. At the entrance to the cave was a pile of small, white bones. Bones!

They scared me so much I wanted to run away, but I made myself scootch down and look into the cave. I could just make out four pups huddled together, their yellow eyes gleaming in the dark. Wolf pups! A little distance away from the pups was a fifth wolf puppy lying on its back, its stiff legs up in the air. It was dead.

Then I heard a familiar whimpering coming from a dark corner of the cave. When I looked closer I saw not two yellow wolf eyes, but one blue eye and one brown eye. It was Silver. As I reached into the cave for him, the largest of the wolf pups snarled at me, baring its sharp teeth. Silver growled at the wolf pup, scaring him away. I scooped Silver up in my arms. He licked my face and nuzzled me. I put him inside my jacket to keep him warm. As Silver snuggled against me I couldn't tell whether the trembling I felt was the puppy or my own heart.

6.

I began to run, afraid that any minute the father or mother wolf might come back. I hoped I was running toward our house. The sun had begun to set and the darkness seemed to be coming to meet me. Mom and Dad and I had often walked here in summer, but now everything that was familiar was covered with snow. I wasn't sure where I was. Silver was growing heavy, but I held on to him and tried not to think what would happen to us if I got lost.

The wind started up, covering my tracks as soon as I made them, so there was no way I could tell if I was going in a circle. You heard stories about this happening to people who wandered into the Alaskan winter. They were never heard from again.

The wind stung my face and the snow crept into my boots and mittens. I had to wriggle my toes and fingers to keep them from growing numb. Suddenly the ground beneath the snow felt spongy. It sucked at my boots and I smelled something dark and musty. I had wandered into the cedar swamp that runs along our land. My dad had warned me to keep out of the swamp because of the deep water-filled holes. Now every step I took scared me. Overhead I saw a large black shadow start up from one of the trees. It was a raven. It spread its dark wings over me and flew off. Even the raven didn't want to be there.

When I finally found my way out of the swamp, I was so tired I didn't think I could take another step. I was about ready to just sink down into the snow and give up when Silver began to whine. There was an answering whine. It was Ruff. She had heard us and was calling to Silver. Silver was squirming so hard I couldn't hold him.

He jumped out of my arms. In a second he was off and running through snow so deep that sometimes all I could see was his feathery tail. I ran after him. All at once there was the light from our windows. Mom was calling. I didn't waste my breath answering. I just ran toward our house and Mom.

7.

The day Dad got home from the Iditarod all the neighbors from miles around came over to hear about the race and congratulate him on taking third place. Even Mary Sue and her folks were there. Mary Sue said, "I saw your dad on television! The camera wasn't very close to him, but I recognized his parka." I could tell she was impressed. She even said maybe she'd race in the

Iditarod like I was going to—until I asked her what she thought her hair would look like after three weeks of snowstorms.

The neighbors stayed all day and everyone was talking at once so there was no time to tell Dad about Silver. Dad had lots of stories about the race. He said it had been forty degrees below zero one night and his and all the dogs' eyelashes had frozen shut. And he talked about seeing things that weren't there. "When you go night after night with almost no sleep," he said, "you start to imagine all kinds of things. I saw hundreds of trees with green leaves, even though I was racing over treeless tundra and it was snowing out."

Later that night, after everyone had gone home, Mom and Dad and I were sitting in front of the fireplace. Silver was curled up asleep on my lap. His legs were twitching in his sleep as though he were dreaming of running a race. "Well, did anything happen here while I was gone?" Dad asked.

That was the question Mom and I had

been waiting for. "Rachel has something to tell you," Mom said. "It's as exciting as your stories about the race." She was grinning.

Dad had that polite look adults give you when they think what you are going to say won't be much. "A wolf stole Silver," I said, "but I got him back." Then Dad really looked interested.

After I had told him the whole story he said, "The mother wolf must have picked up the scent of Ruff and her puppies. She probably stole Silver away to take the place of her own dead pup. In wolf packs, wolves raise one another's pups."

In the distance we could hear a chorus of wolves howling. Silver's ears shot up. He sent up an answering howl. It was half wail and half growl and it nearly made me jump out of my skin. Dad looked really impressed at the noise Silver made. "I can't believe how much that pup has grown since I left," he said.

"That's because you haven't seen Rachel giving him the entire contents of our refrigerator every morning," Mom told him.

"He's brave, too," I said, and told Dad how Silver had scared off the wolf pup when it had tried to bite me.

"I was wrong about Silver," Dad said. "He has the same wolf courage Ruff has. He'll make a fine lead dog."

That night I dreamed I was skimming across the snow. Silver was leading the team of dogs that pulled my sled. We overtook one sled after another until we were out in front, racing toward Nome and the finish line, nothing in front of us but a gray shadow running along, fast as the wind, showing us the way.

ABOUT THE AUTHOR

GLORIA WHELAN lived briefly in Anchorage, Alaska, where she experienced at first hand the Rondy celebration she describes in *Silver*. She says, "I enjoyed the liveliness and enthusiasm people showed during the Rondy. At the same time, I read about the first woman to win the Iditarod, one of the most physically challenging races in the world. These were my inspirations for writing *Silver*, a story about a little girl who dreams of one day racing in the Iditarod."

Gloria Whelan lives with her husband in the woods of northern Michigan, where they see a lot of dog-sled racing right in their own county.

ABOUT THE ILLUSTRATOR

STEPHEN MARCHESI has been drawing since he could hold a crayon, and one of his earliest artistic efforts was making snow sculptures in the wintertime. He has illustrated many books for young people, including *The Glow-in-the-Dark Night Sky Book*.

Stephen Marchesi lives in Bayside, New York.